BURN YOUR
HOUSE DOWN
IN SIX EASY
STEPS

the Awful Tale of Agatha Bilke

Written and Illustrated by

Siân Pattenden

the Awful Tale of
Agatha Bilke

the Awful Tale of Agatha Bilke

Siân Pattenden

✳ SHORT BOOKS

First published in 2006 by

Short Books

15 Highbury Terrace

London N5 1UP

10 9 8 7 6 5 4 3 2 1

A CIP catalogue record for this book
is available from the British Library.

ISBN 1-904977-51-0

First printed in Great Britain by
Bookmarque Ltd, Croydon, Surrey

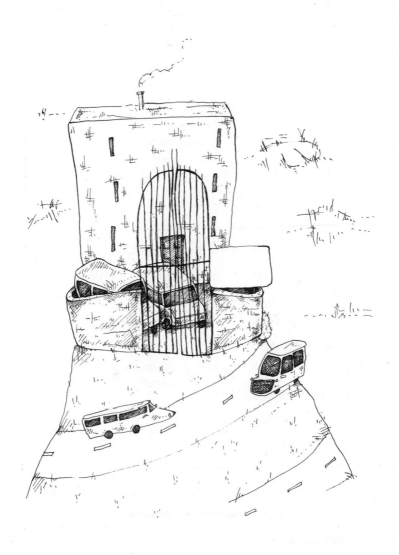

CONTENTS

Prologue

The TreadQuietly Clinic for Interesting Children –

now open for business!

A friendly place which uses creative therapy
to help children sort out their, um, difficulties

Dr Tim and Dr Alan Humphrey are waiting for your call!

Please phone: ███████████████

TreadQuietly

Reprinted courtesy of *Concerned Parents' News*
and the TreadQuietly Clinic

PROLOGUE

Where do you go if you're feeling a bit peaky? The doctor's surgery, and then to the shop to get loads of chocolate. If something more serious happens – perhaps your leg falls off – you might end up in the hospital. But for those of you who have a rather active imagination – a phobia or just a "strange feeling" – you may need to seek more specific help.

This is a story about an awful girl called Agatha Bilke. She found herself in the TreadQuietly Clinic with a group of other children who had problems which were nowhere near as terrible as hers (as far as the future of humanity was concerned), but who were making life difficult all the same. However, little did Agatha realise that when she met Paul Dorey, she would find someone who was, eventually, prepared to fight to keep everyone nice and alive, thank you. Indeed, to fight for the future of humanity.

Almost.

1. AGATHA

Agatha Bilke was a problem child. She liked setting fire to things.

She had faded blonde hair, which was turning a mousy brown colour. It curled at the tips, as if trying to get away from her. Twelve-year-old Agatha was slim and always covered in crumbs or mud; she often wore very large shoes so she could kick people in the shins when she felt like it.

Children are not always known for their good behaviour. Reports of youngsters creating havoc are common and unsurprising. They cover themselves with soot in clean homes or pour viscous liquids onto family pets and then blame someone else. Such activity is greeted with sighs of despair by adults, while the merriment had by the perpetrator has no parallel. There's something really rather warm and appealing about creating chaos, especially if you can get away with it.

But how do we compare the charming, wanton destruction wreaked by a young child with the evil deeds of Agatha Bilke? (And oh, they were evil.) Agatha was long past the age where she could pass off her hobby as "not knowing any better" – for she did know better. And this did not dampen (no pun intended) her delight in seeing solid objects melt under the power of a raging fire. There is nothing more bewitching than looking into the chuckling heart of a flame...

The first time Agatha set fire to something was at a large family gathering, the eve of her elder sister's wedding. Margaret Bilke was a sturdy girl, built like a horse who's watched a lot of wrestling videos. She might have been mistaken for one (a horse not a wrestling video) had she not been an exceedingly good tap-dancer.

Margaret was to marry a simple man who went by the name of Steve, but she was happy. Agatha, on the other hand, thought the match was preposterous: Steve had no interest in dancing. He could not even do robotics. He didn't share her sister's love of pickled onion and marmalade sandwiches, and he was rubbish at Playstation.

Agatha knew that extreme situations required extreme measures. She bundled up her sister's white wedding dress, train, veil, shoes and stockings which had been neatly arranged on the spare-room bed and crept out to the near-by allotments.

She went to her dad's shed, which was filled with pots and shovels, put the bundle inside and struck a match. She watched the shed and its contents go up (quicker than she imagined). It looked triumphant. The flames were deep red in parts, but white or blue in other places, where they were hottest. They fizzed sometimes, like happy friends on a great day out. She had to stand back from the blaze: the heat was incredible.

"That heat is more than incredible," said a voice from behind her. "It is impossible. And I hope it doesn't ruin my potatoes. I've had such a lot of problems already."

Agatha turned to see the worried face of a woman, aged about 70 (although everyone old looks about 70). She was holding out her hand, trying to give Agatha something.

"Go on, take it."

Agatha reached out and a small, gnarled, green potato was placed in her hand. The woman was right – there were a lot of problems with her potatoes.

*She was holding out her hand, trying to give
Agatha something*

"I just can't get them to look right. This one is perfectly edible, but who would want to eat it?"

Agatha agreed; it didn't look very nice. But neither did the fire. Why was the old woman unconcerned by the boisterous flames? Agatha was annoyed that she was not remotely appalled by her behaviour, or frightened for her life.

"When I was growing my leeks, they came out all bendy..." It was clear that this lady was not aware of anything else going on around her. She was as engrossed in her allotment as Agatha was in her desire to ruin her sister's big day.

Any normal child would realise that setting fire to things (including sheds) is very silly, that it causes more harm than is entirely necessary and it doesn't impress old ladies who have difficult vegetable crops. But Agatha realised no such thing. She was so furious that her new friend did not notice what was going on that she set fire to the woman's runner beans. Now, this *did* get the OAP's attention.

"What are you doing to my runners?" she cried, a small bird flying out of her hair. "They were perfect!" she continued. "Oh you awful child!" She jumped up and down and more things fell out of her hair, including a biscuit she'd forgotten to have with a cup of tea.

At this moment a man, who had just arrived to check his cauliflowers, noticed the blaze.

"Did you do this yourself?" he asked Agatha. "You are an awful child!"

Agatha thought she might deny it, but then reasoned that it was much more honest to say nothing at all.

The man quelled the flames with a bucket of water and called the police and fire services, who arrived in a reasonably good amount of time to make sure every bit of the fire was out.

They, too, called her an awful child and rang her parents.

To say that the Bilkes were upset would be very silly. They were devastated. As for her sister, and her intended groom, they were distraught but held the ceremony anyway. Margaret wore an evening dress she'd once worn for a business conference which, she noticed after she'd married the boring Steve, still had a badge that read: "Margaret Bilke, Customer Relations."

Far from Agatha recognising how deeply dreadful and thoroughly wicked her behaviour had been, she simply resolved to be more successful next time and create a bigger blaze. Life was dull without distractions. Her sister would not have found her wedding quite so memorable if Agatha had been a good little girl. The family would just have to get used to the forces of nature; they might even expect it in the future. They could buy some flame-proof cardies and fit metal doors to the house.

Thus disaster struck again, because disaster likes company.

Her sister would not have found her wedding quite so memorable if Agatha had been a good little girl

2. PAUL

Paul Dorey was afraid of toast. If he saw it, he might start feeling sick. Or begin to shake and need a lie-down. He might start turning a very worrying shade of purple.

His mother didn't know why he was afraid of toast. His father didn't know why. The postman was pretty stumped, too. Paul Dorey, 10, just hated the sight, the sound, the feel, the smell and the taste of toast. It had always been so, ever since anyone could remember.

Other families – grinning, jolly, successful families – would have their toaster on the kitchen surface, ready to grill away at a moment's notice. The Doreys had to hide theirs in a cupboard, until Paul told them to get rid of it altogether (all too often the crumbs would fall out onto the floor). When Paul passed a café he would have to look away, in case he saw any grilled slices nestling under scrambled eggs or beans. He found it hard to visit other children, who seemed to eat toast not only for breakfast but sometimes as a snack in the afternoons, too.

Some of them even had sandwich toasters.

His mother knew that other children suffered, or had peculiar whims. Many children in Paul's class, for instance,

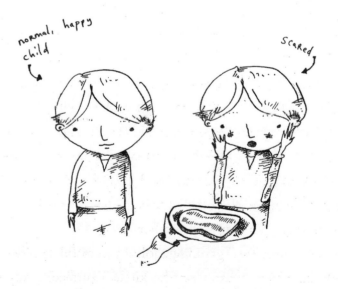

His mother didn't know why he was afraid of toast

had allergies. Some couldn't digest dairy produce properly or got a bit puffy if they ate wheat. Some, it was said, might explode if they even licked a peanut – which seemed very extreme to Mrs Dorey, who enjoyed all sorts of snacks.

Kim Dolphin, so Paul told his mother, had an imaginary friend called Bonce, who would accidentally bang his imaginary head all the time. This was very tiring apparently for all concerned, because Kim would sometimes fall

foul of the same fate. At last year's sports day she had had to be taken home when she'd finished the sack race by colliding with the refreshments table. She blamed it all on Bonce, of course.

In all other respects, Paul was a perfect child. He was quiet, he was mostly tidy, he read books and had regular baths. Paul himself knew he had a problem, and was frustrated by it. If only he could get over this tiny but also peculiarly large obstacle then he would never have anything more to worry about. It wasn't as if he had anything properly, visibly wrong with him, like a lazy eye or an unmanageable knee. He was popular in school, always helping younger children with directions to the newsagents and showing other pupils how to download music legally from the internet.

When he asked his mother what he might be able to do about his phobia, she decided to find a place that might be able to help him. There was nothing mentioned about the future of humanity at that point, in case you were asking.

3. THE DOCTORS HUMPHREY

Newly completed, the TreadQuietly Clinic for Interesting Children had an air of undisputed science – and creative therapy – about it.

Dr Tim Humphrey proudly polished the nameplate on the door which led to the INTERVIEW ROOM.

"When do we get the first batch in?" he asked his brother, Dr Alan.

"First batch?" came the reply. "You mean our eager young case studies, our 'Interesting Children'? They arrive next week – everything must be ready. Have you engaged a nurse?"

Tim blushed. "You know as well as I do that I am

married to my work, and cannot propose to any member of staff."

"I mean have we found someone yet?" Alan was trying to keep calm.

"Oh yes, of course! A delightful woman, goes by the name of Pincer. Very concerned about parking, I must say. I explained she could leave her car out the front."

"Qualified?"

"Well I think she had to have a few goes. Wasn't very good at right-hand turns at first but she soon got the hang of it."

Alan was trying to keep calm

Alan knew only too well that Tim had got the wrong end of the stick. Again. Alan had, of course, asked if Pincer was a fully qualified *nurse*, not *driver*. As he watched Tim endlessly polish the sign on their office door he thought about the years he'd spent working with his brother... and the even-more-years stretched out before them.

Tim reached into his pocket and took out a bag of sweets.

"Marshmallow, bro'?" he asked, as happy as a pony in a cinema.

At this point, Mrs Pincer rang on the doorbell, ready for her first day. Once inside, she gasped at the new interior and in particular the thick carpet which cushioned every footfall.

"It really is delightful, this place," she remarked, smiling broadly at the doctors. "Where can I put my first-aid box?"

Tim had a good feeling about the TreadQuietly Clinic. This was going to be the making of the Humphreys, he was certain. Whoever walked through that door – someone who didn't like pigeons or who needed a light on when sleeping – would be in safe hands with the Humphreys' unique form of treatment. He did not yet know that they would be tested to their limits by the children whose stories will unfold in the next few chapters... For we must

introduce the whole sorry lot of them before we come back
to TreadQuietly and the opening day.

Tim was as happy as a pony in a cinema

4. A BIT MORE ABOUT AGATHA

Agatha lived in a part of Britain known as London. It was full of people, some of them poor, some of them rich. But Agatha did not think about all the people in that most famous of cities. She did not think of urban planning, the transport system, gun crime or inner-city funding. Fair enough, all boring topics. But she should have thought about the emergency services more often because it was those fine people who were at her beck and call.

It was mid-June, and Agatha's parents were going through what they called a "sticky patch". Their hobby – in place of barbershop singing or looking at old things – was being suspicious of each other.

"If we go to into town on Saturday," Mr Bilke might say, "You'll just spend ages looking at rubbish."

Mr Bilke was not referring to his wife's love of contemporary art. He was assuming she would go to the shops and look at things he didn't like. Skirts, pens, mountaineering gear (Mrs Bilke had an unrealised ambition to climb up things)…

"Yes, but you'll go and have one of your *coffees*," Mrs Bilke might reply, bitterness in her heart.

Could coffee really be so awful? Perhaps it meant that Mr Bilke might chat with an attractive lady while ordering his drink, or maybe he had once had a coffee with a man who'd persuaded him to spend a month's wages betting on a horse.

Alas, we shall never know, for the Bilkes' personal problems were never fully revealed to us and it would be

Could coffee really be so awful?

impolite to go prying here in the name of research. We have other, more pressing concerns.

Agatha's next dreadful ploy was to set fire to a boathouse in the dead of night. Twelve canoes were destroyed in half an hour and the wooden building collapsed. It was a spectacle. Flaming timbers leapt off the structure like excitable creatures; the whole scene became animated, alive.

And when the embers were discovered the next morning, Agatha well knew, there'd be a renewed sense of community and lots of jobs for unemployed but highly skilled types who could build a new boathouse and some canoes. She grinned and did a small dance of delight as she felt the heat from the fire on her skin. The dance was not very good, but it didn't matter – no one was watching.

Agatha's gripe with the canoeing world? None. From now on, logic was not part of the process.

Agatha's next dreadful ploy was to set fire
to a boathouse in the dead of night

5. BRENDA AND MIRIAM

Most girls are lovely (Agatha being an exception.) They smile, they laugh, they skip. They put fancy ribbons in their hair, they collect kittens, they sing about helping hungry people. Even the greedy ones.

Some girls are lovely, until they open their ~~mouth~~ big fat gob.

Brenda Keen was such a person. She had golden blonde hair, long arms (useful for hanging from trees) and tried not to spill food down herself, both when eating and at other points (don't ask).

In libraries, in galleries, on the bus and at the swimming-pool, when Brenda entered and opened her ~~mouth~~ big fat gob, people of all ages, colours and specifications would cry out in horror.

"I do believe that an angry whale must be belching close by," someone might say.

"No, I think it could be a motorbike filled with aeroplanes – or perhaps the other way round," an elderly type would probably add.

"That terrible sound must be a lion with a megaphone," another might propose.

Some girls are lovely, until they open their ~~mouth~~ big fat gob

In any case, they all knew where the sound was coming from soon enough.

"IT WOULD BE GREAT IF I COULD RENEW THIS BOOK ON MY LIBRARY CARD!!!!!"

Everyone: "Shhhhhhh!"

"CAN YOU PLEASE GET MY LOCKER OPEN? THIS KEY DOESN'T WORK!!!!"

Everyone: "Shhhhhhh!"

"IF I BURP PERHAPS I CAN START AN EARTH-QUAKE!!!!!"

Everyone else: runs away pretty sharpish.

It might be pertinent to add that Brenda was, as you can imagine, very bad at keeping secrets.

Unlike her sister who was three years younger, Miriam Keen (14) was quiet and very shy. But she too had problems: she was afraid of meteorites. Not afraid of meteorites if she spotted them walking past, on their way to the supermarket or sunbathing in a neighbour's back garden. But afraid of them falling (from space) onto (her head). So fearful was she, that she could only leave the house with a medium-sized piece of corrugated iron strapped to her head — which made her look quite peculiar. She was a tall girl and this added to the problem. If a meteorite were to strike the earth, she reckoned she might get hit first —

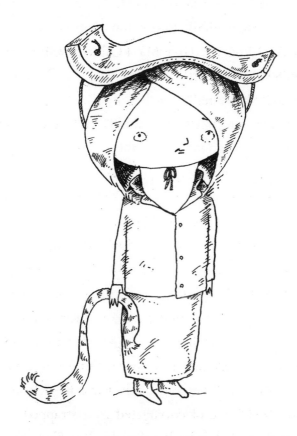

Miriam could only leave the house with a medium-sized piece of corrugated iron strapped to her head

softening the blow for someone like Brenda who was shorter. Miriam had grown her hair very long, thinking that this was more protection. She often wore a scarf, or long boots, or both – for more coverage. As Brenda yelled her way round the world, oblivious to the ears of everyday folk, Miriam felt all too aware of the world turning on its axis, sitting in space, waiting for the rocks of infinity to rain down. All was uncertainty for delicate Miriam Keen.

As you can now imagine, the sisters' parents had to have a long, hard think about where they might seek help for their interesting children.

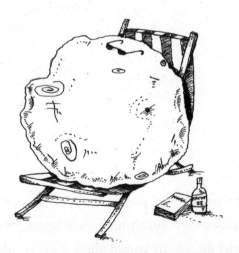

Miriam was not afraid of meteorites if she spotted them sunbathing in a neighbour's back garden

34

6. AND A LITTLE BIT *MORE* ABOUT AGATHA

And so we must rumble ahead to Agatha's next horrific episode. This time, oh bother, she'd taken months to plan it. She would burn down her school, St Heavy Workloads.

As mentioned, Agatha was a very bad child. She was cruel and vicious and mean. She would throw woodland squirrels at people, stamp on her classmates' toes; worse still, she would often pretend to cut off her ears so that other pupils would vomit into their lunch. She didn't have any friends; no parent would allow their child to bring her home for tea – she might scorch the doilies.

Agatha knew that, if she set fire to the school, some people might have to run for their lives and some of the older teachers might get wrapped up in the flames and maybe perish. But she didn't really worry about this, because she was made up of so many evil thoughts and so many evil limbs and so many evil arteries and fiddly, evil blood vessels.

She burned the place down and it wasn't very difficult. She left a Bunsen burner on after her chemistry class. She placed it near a stack of exercise books which was situated next to a bundle of newspapers.

She and her class were outside picking up leaves when they heard the fire alarm. Hundreds of worried school-children and teachers rushed out of the burning building.

Then there was a cry from a window on the third floor.

"Help! Help! Someone get us out of here!"

"Please, our classroom is on fire!" said another, tiny voice.

The Art studio was ablaze. Anatomically incorrect self-portraits were catching alight and setting the easels on fire. Smoke was pouring out of the open windows. Mrs Doctrine, the Art teacher, was busy trying to fashion a ladder out of the material the pupils studied "folds" from. It wasn't long enough.

*Anatomically incorrect self-portraits were catching
alight and setting the easels on fire*

Agatha thought she might see her first casualties.

"Hang on!" shouted Mrs Doctrine brightly. "Oh! Silly me! Silly silly me!" she laughed, as she opened the back door of the studio and told the pupils to walk down the fire escape. "In all that rush I had forgotten we had this exit!! Hee hee!" she giggled. The young artists did not look happy as they raced down the three flights of metal steps.

By this time, everyone was out of the building, except for the headmaster.

"Have you seen Mr Pavlov?" asked the teachers, together, "Where can he be?"

An hour later, he was still nowhere to be seen.

It seemed to Agatha that she might have been the cause of Mr Pavlov's inopportune death. "Ha!" she thought, and smiled. For Agatha, this institution had just received a kick in the teeth, a smack in the mouth, a punch in the cake hole.

7. BARRY

"Barry would like someone to refill his glass of water... if someone would be so kind."

"Barry is not sure whether this channel might be suitable for his age group. Could someone please switch over to BBC1?"

"Barry is wondering whether it isn't just the right time to eat a boil-in-the-bag cod meal. Cod is an endangered fish, but one Barry enjoys nonetheless."

There once was a boy who always spoke of himself in the third person. He had a turned-up nose and wore a shirt and tie with very woolly trousers, even in summer. Guess what he was called?

Rupert! (Only joking.)

Barry had spent his earlier years being mostly normal. Of course, like everyone else, he used the word "I" (as in, "I really am terribly thirsty, mother. Can I have a large glass of elderflower cordial?")

He went to school, he did his homework, he watched television dramas starring actors in frock-coats, set in large country ~~horses~~ houses. Barry Childs (despite his name, he had sophisticated tastes) was a boy who liked home improvement programmes and fresh figs with Greek yoghurt – when the fruit was in season.

Then came the accident.

One day, after cycling up a small grassy knoll in special knee-breeches that his mother had made him for Christmas, Barry fell off his bicycle and onto his head. From then onwards, he referred to himself only as Barry. That was five years ago; the child was now 12.

Barry's mother didn't actually mind – she thought it a charming affection that should be encouraged. She herself was mildly eccentric, wearing nothing but emerald green, carrying her shopping in a cat basket (without a cat in it) and snacking frenziedly on lettuce. There was no Mr Childs. He had left the family when Barry was a mere baby. (N.B. The word "mere" should really read "enormous" as

*There once was a boy who always spoke of
himself in the third person*

Barry had always been colossal for his age. He had once been mistaken for a traffic warden at the age of seven.)

Barry hadn't heard from his father since he left. All he knew was that he'd taken nothing but his trusty bench press, which he exercised on in order to have bigger arm muscles.

"Barry imagines that Mr Childs is doing good some-where, lifting people out of burning buildings, or at least carrying heavy shopping for old ladies."

It was only when Barry started to have trouble at school that Mrs Childs started to worry about him.

"Class is becoming difficult," the son told his dear mother, who was munching on a Little Gem. "Barry is not happy about the type of school-persons he is meeting."

She looked at his black eye.

"They're not so pleased with Barry, by the looks of things," she said. "Let me think about this. I'm sure we can come up with a solution."

Barry's mother herself was mildly eccentric,
carrying her shopping in a cat basket

8. EVEN MORE ABOUT AGATHA BECAUSE WE HAVEN'T FINISHED THIS BIT YET

Agatha was suspected of burning down her school, although she never admitted to it. Her parents did not know what to do with her. They met with a police officer, Inspector Coddles, who told them Agatha was a danger to the public. So they took their daughter (no, not Margaret – Agatha) to the doctor, who recommended a special place for her – the TreadQuietly Clinic.

Although the Bilkes did not want the whole world to know that their youngest daughter was a problem, they had to admit that she was and they trusted the doctor's opinion. They were not to know that she would be in the Clinic with other innocent (albeit somewhat confused) children who would be at the mercy of their evil girl. They were not to know that young Paul Dorey would be tested beyond his powers.

(Mr Pavlov was found alive and well in Hastings, by the way, on the South Coast of England. He had used the opportunity the fire had given him to flee a job he hated and had set up shop as a clairvoyant on the beach. He had always fancied himself as a palm reader and bought a book on it. Whenever he didn't know anything, he made stuff up.)

Mr Pavlov had set up shop as a clairvoyant on the beach

9. THE TREADQUIETLY CLINIC FOR INTERESTING CHILDREN

And so Agatha, Paul, Brenda, Miriam and Barry found themselves at the TreadQuietly Clinic for Interesting Children, all at the same time. Each of them had been sent there in order to be cured of their respective problems. They had all been given a few weeks off school and would receive treatment and tutoring at the Clinic.

Dr Alan Humphrey and Dr Tim Humphrey had practised under the most eminent, bearded psychologists in their field before founding the Clinic (which was not in a field at all, but next to a main road). Their mother had instilled in these men a deep feeling of compassion but no small amount of nosiness. And nosiness is very important for doctors. It helps them get to the bottom of things.

Tim and Alan were committed. That is, committed to their task (because the other "committed" actually means something quite serious and often quite tricky in terms of hospitals etc. and is explained for more, er, stable readers on the back page).

Tim was the most enthusiastic of the pair. As the younger brother, he was excited at the prospect of sharing a clinic with his brother rather than with fusty old men in beards and spectacles.

Alan, on the other hand, was sensible. He was a serious type. Say the brothers were two halves of a football match, the first (Alan) would be quite an earnest and dedicated game; the second (Tim) would be prone to players wandering around, stopping to make a quick cup of tea, pointing to objects in the sky (real and/or imagined) and fainting.

Alan had spent much of his childhood saving Tim from falling out of trees, cars, boxes and bin-liners (don't ask). In adulthood Alan would often restrain Tim (another dreadful and completely accidental reference to mental health hospitals!! Oh no!!! Confound it!! Apologies and don't look on the back page unless you are of sound mind. Ooph! Done it again!) when his flights of fancy went too far.

Yet, together, Alan and Tim were formidable, a "great team", as one of the medical magazines had recently written. Tim benefited from Alan's good sense and Alan relied on Tim's imagination to provide "New Ways for Treatment". For they had invented an entirely new system of therapy. Tim had wanted to be an actor when he was a young boy so he had attended drama classes.

He had pretended to be a tree.

He had tried to feel like he was a chair (with some success: he wouldn't stand up for a whole weekend and remained crouched near the kitchen table).

He had even attempted to get inside the (concrete) mind of a pavement. Hard work.

Ultimately, all these exercises led to "becoming" another person. Tim loved to act; it was a sad day when he hung up his tights and decided to be a doctor instead. But Alan had insisted that an actor's life was tough and that he need-ed to train for a more secure job. For a while, Tim had secretly hoped that one day he would perform again, that he would hang up his stethoscope and pick up those tights again – which were on the same hook under his dressing gown or "goon" as he liked to call it... but that was before he and his brother had invented...

The Humphrey Technique

This was better than acting, thought Tim. This method used those acting skills and put them to even better use: helping children, who were open to unusual and more fantastical things. They would find wonder in the more inventive treatments, Tim reasoned, they would marvel at his props (more of which to come) and their brains, quite frankly, were a lot more malleable.

Of course, some children have problems, just like adults. But, where grown people have years of feeling bad about something and therefore tend to get used to it, children are far more inclined to embrace a new way of thinking in order to understand their condition. (Apart from anything else, Tim thought, it was a

Tim had pretended to be a tree

great excuse to have lots of marshmallows in the place, a treat which he enjoyed after a hard day's therapeutin'.)

The Humphrey Technique was almost all drama-based. It centred around empathy, which means the ability to identify with and understand another person's feelings or difficulties. Empathy can also mean the transfer of your own feelings and emotions to an object such as a painting, or even a lampshade (if it's a nice one).

Empathy, for Dr Tim and Dr Alan, was the vital clue to an individual's success. It created a connection with others, the very reason for the soul to exist. How could a "problem" child ever hope to learn to be a caring, creative adult if he or she wasn't taught about how others felt? After all many qualities are learnt – they do not happen by accident or instinct. Empathy is a little like dancing, thought Tim, some are better at it than others, but everyone can learn to boogie.

So, if a child was afraid of something (i.e. toast, meteorites), the Doctors Humphrey would enable them to *become* it – hadn't Tim felt so often like a piece of furniture? Thus the patients would eventually learn to understand their problem and all fear would dissolve away. This technique was perfect for young patients who had phobias.

Empathy can also mean the transfer of your own feelings
and emotions to an object such as a lampshade
(if it's a nice one)

The children shouted (i.e. Brenda) or talked of them-selves in a silly way (i.e. Barry) would understand how others felt when listening to them. They would become someone (or something, perhaps – the possibilities were endless) outside of themselves and see sense.

What of the children who displayed quite unbearable, compulsive behaviour? The sort that no right-thinking child would ever dream of doing, i.e. Agatha Bilke?

The Humphrey Technique would – of course – put them in the position of their victim, they would then see what effect their actions had and eventually stop. The brothers were aware that this was the most difficult task. ~~Criminal~~ Psychologically complex types – young and old – often found it difficult to empathise. (Tim had seen this in a thriller novel, which he'd read from cover to cover, it was excellent, a real page-turner.) But with his knack for creating the right atmosphere and the new Clinic, which boasted 17 rooms and off-road parking, the Humphreys knew that they could transform the lives of many children for years to come. They only had to prove themselves with this first batch of five and then they were away.

Medals, trophies, their own psychology show on BBC1 and then the cover of the *Radio Times*… Tim fantasised about the glories that awaited them. He found it best not to do this while he was reversing in the carpark. The Clinic's nurse, Mrs Pincer, had not been happy about the dent in her Lancia.

Neither Tim nor Alan stopped to think that someone as horrifying, as wicked and as awful as Agatha might be rolling up to the front gates any time now. If they had done so, they might have had a less positive outlook on the future… the future of humanity.

Mrs Pincer had not been happy about the dent in her Lancia

10. INSIDE TREADQUIETLY

"Welcome to TreadQuietly," greeted Mrs Pincer. "Please, parents, say your goodbyes – you'll be able to visit your children in a week's time."

Despite the fact that it had just opened, the Clinic building was very old. It had been converted from a Victorian mansion. It stood on its own, at the top of a busy thoroughfare, just by a roundabout.

Mrs Pincer was a portly lady, with rosy cheeks and white hair scraped into a bun. She shuffled her feet over the gravel, impatiently, as if she were trying to polish the pebbles with the soles of her shoes.

"You will be OK, won't you?" sniffed Mrs Childs,

hugging her son tightly.

"Barry will be just fine, mama," he said, trying to wriggle free.

"What do you think they have for breakfast? Toast?" whispered Paul to his mother, nervously.

"It's all right, they know all about your condition," replied Mrs Dorey. "This place is a centre of medical excellence. It says so in the brochure."

As the other parents sobbed and gurgled, Agatha Bilke's parents were, to be quite frank, relieved to see her go.

"Come on everyone," the nurse called to the other children. "It's time for the tour around the house and grounds."

"WHERE EXACTLY ARE WE?" shouted Brenda to Mrs Pincer, as the saddened parents got into their cars. "ARE WE IN TOWN, OR OUT OF TOWN IN THE LAND OF ADVENTURE??"

"Oh, we are very much out of town, young lady," said Mrs Pincer, who did not appear to be alarmed by Brenda's loud voice. "And this is certainly the land of adventure." Mrs Pincer grinned, her cheeks grew rosier. She led them upstairs and showed them the dormitory.

The new patients ogled the interior. Paul was especially impressed that the walls were freshly painted, the flooring newly laid and that light shone brightly in through the windows. Beside each bed was a reading lamp and a selection of books. It was perfect.

"THIS IS MUCH NICER THAN MY BEDROOM AT HOME!!" yelled Brenda.

As they walked downstairs, they passed some doors which were bolted shut. These doors were not white but a glossy, beetle-back black.

"What's behind there?" asked Miriam, adjusting her corrugated-iron hat, in case there were any forceful meteorites waiting to come out.

"Those are the treatment rooms," said Mrs Pincer.

The children looked at each other; the doors were so heavy, so dark. They shivered – all apart from Agatha who snarled, "Ooh, I'm scared." But of course she wasn't scared in the slightest.

Paul looked at her. He had never met someone so ungrateful in his life. They had been given the opportunity of top-notch treatment in this brand-new clinic, by promising young doctors, and all this girl could be was sarcastic. But Mrs Pincer said nothing and they continued to descend.

They passed a small window on the landing.

"Barry would like to know what all those fridges are doing piled up in the back garden."

"I'm afraid that's the council's property," said Mrs Pincer. "It is a place that is used to store old refrigerators before they are properly disposed of. They can be an environmental menace if dumped. It's so good they have somewhere to store them now."

"Barry would like to know what all those fridges are doing piled up in the back garden," said Barry

The children looked very seriously at one another, again, remembering their debt to the world's upkeep.

"Is there a garden?" asked Paul. "It would be good to have somewhere to play."

"There's always the carpark," said Mrs Pincer, who was an optimistic, feel-good sort of lady. "I find children with a little imagination can make the most of any situation if they try hard enough."

At this, Agatha gave a loud tut. Paul turned to Mrs Pincer, who still said nothing but smiled her way down-stairs. They reached the basement and walked up to a white double door. It, too, had been newly painted.

"And this, my dears, is the refectory," said Mrs Pincer. "Monsieur Pipette is our French chef; he'll be cooking all your meals."

The children gasped as she led the way in. There were three white tables, a small serving area and a kitchen behind. Although there were no windows, everything was white, gleaming, as if they were in a snowdrift. It was so new, so optimistic. But the most marvellous thing was, there were bowls full of marshmallows everywhere.

"You'll find that after treatments you'll be entitled to a large handful of marshmallows," said Mrs Pincer. "There are always plenty stocked in the cupboards. Dr Tim is a big fan.

He and Dr Alan will be looking after you during your stay."

The children looked at each other for the third time, but their faces were not serious anymore, they were filled with feverish delight.

"I'm sure you'll all be very pleased with the Humphrey Technique."

The children nodded, even though none of them had a clue what Mrs Pincer might mean. They had no understanding – for how could they? – of what might lie ahead of them. They were just pleased they had come to a place which had free sweets. Agatha was pleased because she had espied a box of cooks' matches, right by the kitchen hob. Just like any other matches, but for the fact they are longer, they make setting fire to objects very easy indeed. She looked at her fellow patients: gleeful, hopeful. Not one of them would ever stand up to her. Would they?

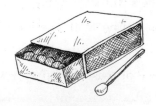

Agatha was pleased because she had espied
a box of cooks' matches, right by the kitchen hob

11. TREATMENT ONE: PAUL

Monday morning, and while Mrs Pincer was teaching the other children crochet, Paul had his first meeting with the doctors in the INTERVIEW ROOM. It was, again, startlingly white. Every surface looked polished, exact. The doctors themselves were wearing pristine white coats and they were scribbling notes. Paul thought this might be what sitting in the inside of a fridge would be like.

"So, it's any piece of toast that gives you the wobblers?" asked Tim.

"Yes," gulped Paul.

"French toast? Beans on toast? Grilled ciabatta?

Crispbreads?" asked Alan, ticking boxes as he spoke.

Paul looked a little green. He nodded, very slowly. Then he threw up over Tim's shoes.

"Sorry."

"That's quite all right," said Tim brightly, enthused by Paul's violent reaction, while Alan swiftly ticked a large box at the bottom of his notes. "We're sure we've got just the thing. We've spent all night constructing it."

They led Paul out of the INTERVIEW ROOM and along a corridor, thick red carpet under their feet, up a small flight of stairs and to the end of another corridor. Paul had certainly not seen this part of the Clinic when they had been given the tour. The building was much bigger than he had thought; from the outside he wouldn't have dreamed that you could fit this much in. Every door he passed was beetle-back black, until he got to the final one. On it was a sign that read, THE GRILL ROOM.

It was at this point that Paul started to feel the tension at the back of his neck. Some might say that "alarm bells started ringing". The problem was, no alarm bells started ringing, nothing happened like that at all. He knew the other children were in the Clinic somewhere, blissfully ignorant of his fearful journey, making pompom hats.

The doctors noticed Paul shrink away.

"There's nothing to be scared of," said Tim, as he turned the handle and walked forwards, guiding him in. Alan locked the door behind them and Paul found himself standing in front of a huge object. It loomed, bulky and fearsome. It was shiny and square-ish.

"What's in that tent?" asked Paul. "Toast??" It is absolutely needless to say here that Paul was anxious, worried, concerned and a little wary. Yes he wanted to be cured of his preposterous phobia, but he was not prepared to do just *anything* to achieve that aim. And he would definitely not sleep in a tent full of toast, that's for sure. No siree. No madam-ee.

"I'd like to leave, now," said Paul, who would have been sick if he hadn't been already.

Tim was firm. "Why Paul, this is the height of therapy! You will be a very famous chap if — *when* — this works. This is not a tent, Paul, it is a replica of a giant toaster."

Paul had never heard of such a thing. He had never seen

a giant, he had never heard of them eating toast and he wondered if Dr Tim and Dr Alan had severely lost their marbles, if you can severely lose marbles that is, and not just lose them in an ordinary way.

"My lad," continued Alan. "This is the treatment of the future. You hate toast – worse still, you are frightened of it. If you want to rid your fear, you must *become* it. Then you will know how it feels to be a harmless bit of grilled bread. You will be cured... in a few weeks. Then we'll all be happy."

"It may look like a tent to you, but once we lower you in, you'll love it," said Tim. "And then, it's marshmallow time!"

Paul was not convinced, but he had no choice but to follow the doctors' wishes. He was lowered into the "toaster". He stood so that his head popped out. He felt, reporters were told later, a little bit uncomfortable.

The doctors stood back. From this height, Paul could see more of the room. It looked like a well-presented, high-ceilinged, Victorian drawing-room. It was covered in posters, like a teenager's bedroom... but they were not pictures of racing cars or pop stars, they were pictures of things like fried eggs, sausages and beans.

When Paul looked back at the doctors, they had

vanished. Then he heard music. He was just starting to feel faint when Dr Tim Humphrey walked back into the room, wearing a teapot costume.

"Don't be afraid!" he called through the spout. "You're with your friends!!"

Paul tried to feel like a piece of toast. He closed his eyes

Paul stood so that his head popped out.
He felt a little bit uncomfortable

and wrinkled his nose. He tried to concentrate until his knees started to feel warm.

He opened his eyes and saw the teapot swaying from side to side. If it had been a real teapot, thought Paul, it would have spilt half the tea.

"I am a teapot and I am your friend!" Tim was singing

enthusiastically. "You are just a lovely piece of delicious toast. Nothing to be afraid of! Something to enjoy!" The song did not rhyme.

"Stop! Stop!" cried Paul. "I think I'm going to pass out!"

Alan rushed up to the giant toaster, climbed up and pulled Paul out. He did look rather purple.

"He is all right, isn't he?" asked the teapot.

"I think so," replied Alan. "We'll give him a debriefing and then it's time for dinner."

"A what?" asked Tim.

"Dinner. It's a meal you have in the evening."

"No, silly," said Tim. "You said 'de-beefing'. I didn't know there was any beef. There's a picture of some saus–"

"I said debriefing, you soppy lump," barked Alan. "It means we'll talk through the whole event to make sure Paul is fine." He sighed and said to Paul, "You'll be OK."

Paul nodded slowly. This therapy was going to take a long time.

"*I am a teapot and I am your friend!*"
Tim was singing enthusiastically

12. POMPOM HATS

Barry was enjoying crochet lessons the most and his hat was the best in the group by far. He had been able to weave in silver and gold thread as he worked the yarn and he had found some ribbon, too.

Miriam had forgone the yarn in favour of metal wire, which she reasoned gave her added protection under the piece of corrugated iron she already had on her head.

"MRS PINCER!" hollered Brenda. "AGATHA DOESN'T SEEM TO BE FOLLOWING THE RULES!"

Agatha was making what looked like two very small hats, suitable only for dolls or hamsters.

"Now, now," Mrs Pincer walked up and put her hands on

*Barry was enjoying crochet lessons the most and his
hat was the best in the group by far*

Agatha's shoulders, which the child did not like. "That's not a suitable size for a hat, is it?"

"These are not hats," replied Agatha. "They're earmuffs."

"And why earmuffs, child?" asked Mrs Pincer, softly.

"So I don't have to listen to Brenda shouting all the time." Agatha took a piece of wire and started to make a headband to fix the earmuffs on to. "Why can't we bake a cake or something?"

Mrs Pincer had been warned about Agatha and looked her straight in the eye.

"You well know that *certain* people are not allowed in the kitchen area, for *certain* reasons they are not allowed near the hob or oven. And they are definitely not allowed matches to light such appliances. Accidents can happen and we don't want any of that at TreadQuietly. You are here to recover, Agatha."

"If Miriam is allowed to make a hat from metal wire and Barry has put ribbons in his, can I make one using strips of paper?"

Mrs Pincer was pleased to see Agatha showing an interest. But she mistook one interest (hats) for another (evil deeds).

"Of course, Agatha. You do that. Creativity is an important part of development, and recovery."

"I could make a hat for Paul, seeing as he isn't here…"

"Why not? A delightful thought," said Mrs Pincer, who went to get a big bowl of marshmallows, seeing as everyone was doing so well. She didn't stop to think that Agatha had never, ever had a delightful thought.

13. PAUL RELATES HIS TREATMENT

"It must be called TreadQuietly, because the corridors leading to the treatment rooms are covered in thick red carpet," said Paul. "You can't hear your own footsteps – or anyone else's, no matter how much you stamp."

The children were agog. They sat on their beds in the dormitory, each wearing the hat they had made, Paul in the paper one Agatha had crafted. But Agatha was not part of the conversation, she was reading a book about the Melting Of The Arctic Ice Shelf instead. (A shelf-help book, if you like).

"Barry knew there had to be something in the name 'TreadQuietly'! Soft carpets! Well Barry never."

"And what happened in your treatment room?" asked Miriam, a little shakily.

"Dr Humphrey dressed up as a teapot," said Paul.

"WHAT??" yelled Brenda. "ARE YOU FRIGHTENED OF TEAPOTS?"

Agatha read a book about the Melting Of
The Arctic Ice Shelf. (A shelf-help book, if you like)

"No," said Paul. "I'm not very good with toast."

"Really?" asked Barry. "Little bits of toast? Barry is not scared of toast at all. Quite the opposite."

"NEITHER AM I!"

"That's very strange," said Miriam. "Toast isn't heavy and it doesn't have sharp edges. It doesn't even fall from the sky."

"YOU'VE KEPT VERY QUIET, AGATHA," said Brenda, who hadn't. "COME ON, JOIN IN!! PAUL'S BEEN DANCING WITH TEAPOTS!"

"I can't hear you," replied Agatha, who obviously could. "I have my new earmuffs on."

Miriam whispered something to Barry. Who whispered that something to Paul. Who whispered that something to Brenda. Who said:

"MY SISTER SAYS SHE SAW YOUR PICTURE IN THE PAPER! SO YOU LIKE TARTAN FLIES THEN?"

"What?" asked Agatha, bemused but still superior. Miriam nudged Barry, who nudged Paul, who whispered again to Brenda.

"OH! YOU LIKE STARTING FIRES!" Brenda looked a little uncomfortable. "I HOPE YOU'RE NOT GOING TO START ONE HERE! THE DOCTORS WILL BE VERY UPSET IF YOU DO!"

Agatha didn't say anything, but stomped up to Paul and took the crocheted paper hat from his head.

"Oi, that's mine!" he whimpered.

"It's not any more," said Agatha. "I made it and I'm having it back."

"You're a big bully, you know," said Paul, trying to stand up to the terrible youngster.

"So what?" cried Agatha. "It beats being a big drip like you."

She stuck her evil face in front of his, as if she was looking through a pane of glass. "Frightened by a teeny-weeny bit of TOAST, are we?"

She spat the word "toast", then looked very pleased with herself as Paul ran off to vomit, leaving the other children looking horrified. They had never imagined a young girl behaving so badly.

"What's all this shouting?" Mrs Pincer caught Paul as she came in. He was sick over her shoes.

"Oh dear!" she exclaimed. "You must have had a difficult first day, Paul. I'll get you cleaned up. Come along. The rest of you, it's bedtime. Silence from now on. Goodnight, children!"

Mrs Pincer switched off the light and took Paul to be cleaned up.

Agatha lay awake thinking. Her first test had produced promising results. She had carefully crafted a very flammable hat in front of the nurse – without comment – and now she had reclaimed it. She had also managed to collect some pencils, a roll of toilet paper and some cotton-wool balls. Yes, she would have plenty of opportunity to create a bit of amusement for herself at TreadQuietly before she unfolded her big plan. Paul Dorey was the easiest to wind up and she had such fun watching him squirm. Satisfied with the day's events, she fell into a heavy, peaceful sleep.

When he got to bed, Paul lay awake thinking, too. He wondered what on earth that treatment had been about. He had tried hard to become a harmless slice of toast and he

Agatha had carefully crafted a very flammable hat and managed to collect some pencils, a roll of toilet paper and some cotton-wool balls

had failed. And, as soon as Agatha had mentioned toast, he had quivered like a buffalo who has just spotted someone wearing a pair of moccasins. He tried to sleep, to dream of things that weren't grilled bread or an evil girl: ice cream, polar bears, toothpaste. It was no use, he was awake. Some would call it wide awake, but it didn't feel very wide, it was small, narrow and not at all pleasant. He hardly slept at all that night.

14. DISASTER STRIKES AGAIN, OR RATHER, AGATHA DOES

At eight o' clock the next morning Mrs Pincer heard more noise coming from the children's dormitory.

"Aaaargh! Help! Noooo!"

Paul had tried to remain calm. He had tried to imagine that the two slices of buttered toast at the bottom of his bed were his friends. He had even tried to conjure up the image of Dr Humphrey dressed as a teapot. It was useless, Paul simply panicked at this dastardly, if not extremely horrendous, prank.

"How did they get there?" fretted the nurse, picking up the slices in front of the trembling child. "Oh you poor little angel, I'll go and get you some marshmallows."

Paul was beginning to realise that he would have to endure weeks of Dr Tim dressed up as a teapot.

Of course, Agatha was behind the stunt, but he had not expected her to be so relentless. Would he ever have a moment's peace? As the other children ran to get Paul a sick bucket and some towels, Agatha sat on her bed, making faces at him.

Mrs Pincer marched to the INTERVIEW ROOM to speak

Paul had tried to imagine that the two slices of buttered toast at the bottom of his bed were his friends

to the two doctors, one of whom was wondering where his two slices of toast had got to.

"I think you should be dealing with Agatha immediately," said Pincer, almost strict but not really. "She has the greatest need for treatment right now."

"But more importantly, Mrs Pincer," said Dr Tim. "I think a certain someone forgot my toast this morning..."

"Yes, but Agatha —"

"Woman!" he shouted. "All very well your concern about our patients, but a man can't go to work on an empty stomach. You must remember in the future, or I'll have to look elsewhere for staff."

Mrs Pincer blushed at Dr Tim's speech, maybe because it was entirely without sensitivity or indeed fact. Dr Alan had to step in — not literally, of course: he was already in the right spot.

"Mrs Pincer did not forget your blessed toast. Agatha stole it to frighten Paul."

"Oh." Tim looked a little rueful. He started to look through his notes intently in order to move on — not literally, of course: he did not need to go anywhere.

"But we've got Barry and Miriam down for today," he said. "The rooms are already prepared. It will ruin the schedule if we chop and change now."

"And after this morning, Paul will need a top-up session," sighed Alan, who was already quite tired and it was only nine in the morning.

"The only thing we can do, Tim, is split up," he continued. "You deal with Barry and Miriam, I'll see Agatha then Paul. Mrs Pincer is right: she must be seen. It's a lot more serious than we thought."

Tim nudged Alan. "You know what to do if it all goes wrong? Give her a marshmallow! They'll cheer anybody up, they will."

Alan looked at his brother but didn't envy his simplicity. He knew Agatha was a difficult child, but he had not expected her to start picking on the other children as soon as she got here. Mrs Pincer had told them what a delightful hat she'd made for Paul and they had all felt a false sense of security, thinking Agatha was settling in well with the other patients. Of course, they had heard all about Agatha from her parents and the local fire brigade, but they had no experience of just how truly awful she was. The Doctors Humphrey believed that therapy would save the world. They didn't realise that Agatha didn't want to be treated; that she was happy just as she was.

14¹/₂. A LITTLE BIT MORE ABOUT PAUL ACTUALLY

Now, getting a gang of like-minded people together to hatch a plan is hard at the best of times. Fortunately, Paul was with similar types at the Clinic. Barry, Brenda and Miriam had seen him being humiliated by Agatha, and were almost as shocked as he was.

They all knew that she must not do this again.

But how could one innocent child help another to behave a little less like a ~~psychopath~~ very disturbed young lady?

There was one main problem: Agatha was not scared of anything. Whereas the other patients were filled with self-doubt and were fully aware that their heads did not seem to work like most others, Agatha was completely self-assured. She loved being awful. She revelled in it. What on earth can you do with someone like that? They are almost impervious to reason and certainly won't respond to being threatened with an illegal but reassuringly heavy implement. But, yes, something had to be done.

Paul thought about what he could do. He thought again. It really was quite difficult.

He felt a bit depressed.

You can understand it, really.

Any one of us would be. (Especially seeing as we're nearly halfway through and we haven't stopped this terrible volcano of a human being from wreaking havoc. And it's raining outside, and a bit windy.)

Paul decided the best plan was to ask what the other children thought when he saw them in the refectory next.

Censored picture of a heavy implement

15. TREATMENT TWO: BARRY

"Barry would like to know, before he goes in, what sort of treatment he might be receiving. Just to be prepared."

"Just you wait and see, Barry," said Alan. "Now tell me, since this accident on the bicycle, you've not used the word 'I'."

"No, Barry has not."

"Even when you are very angry?"

"Barry doesn't get very angry."

"Or when you are incredibly upset?"

"Barry would only say, 'Barry is a little bit upset now.'"

"Would Barry like a marshmallow?" asked Tim.

"Barry would."

"Darn!" thought Tim. "I thought he'd fall for that one."

"Are you sure this is all going to work?" asked the boy. "Barry saw Paul get upset over the toast in his bed this morning. He didn't seem very cured."

Alan tried to restrain himself. Children were so cynical these days.

"It takes time, Barry Childs, it takes time. Dr Tim will conduct your therapy this morning. I have to deal with Miss Bilke."

Barry and Tim walked along that same rich red carpet and up to the treatment rooms. This time, they stopped at a different black-painted door. A sign was pinned on it, MIRROR ROOM.

Barry bit his lip.

"Come along," said Tim. "Don't be afraid."

This time, they stopped at a different black-painted door. A sign was pinned on it: MIRROR ROOM

16. LUNCHTIME

"So no one dressed up as a teapot?" The children quizzed Barry on his treatment as they ate M. Pipette's shepherd's pie.

"Barry only saw a room full of mirrors. It was like the fairground, all different sizes and shapes. In one, Barry looked very fat and in another Barry had very thin legs. And in another, Barry looked like he was gyrating."

At this, Brenda giggled. LOUDLY.

"Then the mirrors started talking," said Barry, nodding with the expression of a boy who had now seen it all. He was still wearing the hat he had made the day before, a hat which had now seen it all.

"What did the mirrors say?" asked Miriam.

"Well, all Barry could hear was a mysterious whisper that sounded as if it had been carried along with the wind, although there was none. Things like, 'This is you. You are me.' Then from behind another, 'I am you. Who do you see? Who are you?' To which Barry obviously replied, 'Barry is Barry, Dr Humphrey.' For Barry guessed that it was he who was pretending to be the mirrors talking."

Brenda gulped. A normal person gulping, you'd hardly hear it. This gulp was more like a drain being unblocked. "GURRRRUUULLLFFPHURGHUPP!"

"Don't you think it's odd that you cannot refer to yourself as 'I'?" asked Miriam seriously, ignoring her sister (which had taken years of practice).

"Not really," answered Barry.

The children were keen to discuss Barry's experience. They were all intrigued by the Humphrey Technique and excited to be the first patients to receive the soon-to-be celebrated method. They were pleased, too, that Agatha was spending the whole day with Dr Alan, receiving emergency therapy. Wasn't it nice when Agatha wasn't here? Paul knew it was time to rally together.

"Friends," he started, not sure whether this was a good word to begin with, but using it nonetheless. "Am I right in

**"WE SHOULD THINK OF A PLAN TO DEAL
WITH AGATHA OURSELVES!"**

thinking that Agatha's temporary absence has made us
jollier, calmer and more reflective as people?"

"MORE REFLECTIVE?" yelled Brenda. "YES."

"Agatha is a bit of a wrong 'un," said Barry. "She winds
everyone up."

"I agree," said Miriam, adjusting the straps on her metal
headgear. "I only hope the Doctors Humphrey can treat her
quickly."

"But what if they can't?" asked Paul. "You've all seen how

I still have my, er, problem. What if Agatha is just as dreadful for weeks on end? How will we cope?"

"YOU MEAN WE SHOULD THINK OF A PLAN TO DEAL WITH HER OURSELVES?!"

"Barry thinks Paul should at least get his own back."

"WE COULD TELL THE DOCTORS THAT SHE'S ON A DIET AND SHE WON'T GET ANY FOOD!"

"That won't work," said Miriam. "She'd steal ours."

"If it were down to Barry, Barry would try and give her a lethal dose of 'flu so she'd be incapacitated for a few weeks."

"And where would we get a dose of 'flu?" asked Paul. "It also sounds a bit criminal…"

"We could hypnotise her!" squeaked Miriam. "Does anyone know how? I saw it on the television once and it was very impressive."

Around the table, everyone shook their head. Their amassed talents were slim. There was someone who shouted, someone who could only refer to himself in the third person, another scared of toast and a last one who thought that big rocks would rain down on her from the sky at any minute.

They each looked at each other. This wasn't a crack team.

"We haven't got anything going for us at all!" said Miriam, sinking into her chair. Her metal hat drooped a little bit. "Agatha is... invincible."

"But..." said Paul. "If the doctors could help...?"

"Children!" Nurse Pincer walked in and started clapping her hands. "Time for treatments! Miriam, you're with Dr Tim – just go upstairs and follow the signs. Agatha's still with Dr Alan. Everyone else, we can get on with some home economics."

Mrs Pincer grinned a broad grin at M. Pipette in the kitchen. He smiled back, thinking how her eyes looked as blue as a mountain stream. Pipette had been made nervous by Agatha's behaviour that morning. He had been warned about matches, but not that she might steal the toast from Dr Humphrey's breakfast tray. He didn't know what she would get up to next. He would have to be more vigilant in the future and would now assure Mrs Pincer that he would do all he could to help.

Kind, gentle Mrs Pincer.

*M. Pipette smiled back, thinking how Mrs Pincer's
eyes looked as blue as a mountain stream*

17. TREATMENT THREE: MIRIAM

"And this is the WEATHER ROOM..." Dr Tim Humphrey opened a large black door to reveal an enormous space, more than double the size of the MIRROR ROOM. The ceiling was extraordinarily high and hanging from it was an elaborate harness, the type you would see at the circus. The floor seemed to be covered in plastic grass.

"All we have to do," said Tim, the most excited that Miriam had seen him, "is to strap you in and watch you go! But first, you must take off that piece of corrugated iron from your head. And the metal pompom hat underneath."

Miriam looked afraid. "But I can't."

"Of course you can. Come on now." Tim was firm.

"I absolutely cannot take either of them off. They protect me."

"Look, Miriam," said Tim, wilfully. "You are going to be a meteorite, then you will understand what they are like and you will never be afraid. In that harness, you are going to swing down to earth. A meteorite cannot under any circumstances wear a hat. No rock has ever worn a hat."

"But I'm wearing clothes. And boots. Meteorites don't wear them either."

Miriam had a point.

"It's just that – oh, OK, wear your hat then. As long as it doesn't fall off and hit me or my props."

They both walked to the far end of the room (which was far, far away), climbed up a long ladder onto a small but stable platform, and Tim fitted her harness and climbed back down.

"Don't worry about a thing," he called up to her. "You're perfectly safe. All you have to do is leap off when I reappear."

A few minutes later, he appeared from behind a curtain, wearing a sunhat, shorts and tennis shirt. He wheeled a small privet hedge over the grass and carried a pair of shears. He began to hum and started clipping the fence, as if he were an unsuspecting man going about his own

"Don't worry about a thing," Tim called up to her.
"You're perfectly safe"

business in the comfort of his back garden.

"Just see me as an unsuspecting man going about my own business," he called up. "You are a meteorite. You will swing at me and I shall look slightly surprised, but you will see that I am not terrified by you at all. In fact, I may start taking notes in my 'Outer Space' jotter, such is my interest."

Miriam had to remind herself that this would make her feel better. She had to *feel* like a meteorite. She would storm down to earth, just a lump of matter from the stars and land with a thud on the grass. Everything would be fine.

"Excuse me, Dr Tim?" she called from the platform, 15 metres from the floor. "What happens when I land? I don't want to break a leg."

The doctor didn't hear. He was trimming the hedge with tiny movements, looking absorbed in his work. It was at this point that Miriam relied on her sister's tactics: shouting.

"DR TIM!!" She hollered, the force of her words making the platform vibrate. "WHAT HAPPENS WHEN I LAND???"

Dr Tim looked up, startled. "Oh, er, it's fine. Under this plastic grass layer is a soft, flexible floor covering that will cushion you. I spent all last night testing this, there's not a bruise on me."

"Deep breath," Miriam told herself. "I have to conquer this thing."

On a count of three, she leapt off the platform and swung down to Dr Tim.

Of course, Tim Humphrey had tested the equipment. He had swung from the ceiling, secure in the harness and landed safely on the cushioned surface below. Everything was in working order. What he hadn't actually done was test his own reactions to someone swinging down at him at breakneck speed. He didn't realise how frightening it would be; how Miriam would look like a terrible bird gone wrong.

"Oooooooorrrghhhh!!!!!" was Tim's initial reaction. His next was: "WATCH OUT!"

Miriam saw the doctor panic and duck down. This was not the "calm man casually watching a meteorite fall" that both had expected. And, instead of hitting the ground smoothly and coming to rest, Miriam continued her course, swinging right back up again at the far end of the room, as if she were a pendulum on an enormous clock.

"Stop!" said the doctor, waving his shears around, which wasn't very wise. "Come back!"

"I can't stop!" shouted Miriam at the terrified Humphrey

Miriam did come back, right back towards Tim and the privet hedge.

"I can't stop!" shouted Miriam at the terrified Humphrey. Her metal hat fell on the soft grass.

It was here that Tim realised his fatal flaw. He had not accounted for the fact that Miriam was at least a foot smaller than him. Where he had been able to touch the ground and then land, Miriam could not do the same. She kept on swinging until Tim realised the only thing he could do was try and grab her as she flew past. He managed to do this on the third attempt and she fell onto the grass and started crying.

"That was awful!" she sniffed. "Where's my hat? I need to put it back on."

"Here," replied Tim brightly, handing her the piece of corrugated iron and trying to be cheerful. "But I'm sure you felt great, swinging above the earth. All power to you, Miriam. You will have command over your fear!"

The poor child looked at him. Tim really did believe he – *they* – had been triumphant. She fastened the metal onto her head. Yes, she must have the will to wish herself better but she doubted she would be able to feel that she was a friendly meteorite for a while. For a long while.

18. PAUL'S POINTLESS TOP-UP SESSION

It was the evening, and the children still had not seen Agatha. She had spent all that time with Dr Alan and no one knew what sort of treatment she was having. The patients sat in the refectory, eating a lovely dinner of sausage and mash that they had made during the home economics lesson.

"Barry thinks that perhaps Agatha is being told off for what she did to Paul this morning."

"MAYBE SHE'S HAVING TO WATCH THE DOCTOR DRESSED UP AS A BARBEQUE!" (Brenda had been given a small pre-supper treatment when Tim had performed the part of a local library.)

"I do hope for her own sake she's not having to fly through the air," said Miriam, who had not quite recovered from her own ordeal.

"No, I did not have to fly, nor did I watch a barbeque and I was not told off." Agatha walked into the dining area and sat next to the children. "I'm famished," she said, with a certain glee. "Where's my sausage and mash?"

Pipette, making sure his matches were in sight, served up the food.

Dr Tim walked in. "Ah, Miss Bilke, had a good day?"

"Highly effective," she replied.

"Good, good. Have you seen my brother?"

"I'm afraid the last time I saw him was when I was having my treatment," said Agatha.

"Ah – hm. I'd better have another look. Perhaps he's in the carpark. It's just Paul needs a quick top-up treatment after tea."

Tim went to look for Alan. Calm, sensible Alan. Surely he couldn't have wandered off somewhere? Whose turn was it to go shopping? Had he accidentally walked into the fridge mountain at the back of the house and been unable to get back out?

"Alan!!!" cried Tim as he wandered out of the ~~mouse~~ house. "Alaaan! Paul needs his top up!!"

After half an hour's fruitless search — if he had been searching for fruit it would have been a double disaster — Tim saw Paul himself in the INTERVIEW ROOM. Alan would be along soon, he hoped.

"So, you're still afraid of toast?" Dr Tim was walking around the office, hands in the pockets of his white coat.

Paul nodded.

"Well, we never said it would be quick. When you were confronted by the toast in your bed this morning, could you not, er, remember being a slice only the day before?"

"I tried, but I just saw the… the stuff," Here Paul looked a little pale. "And it made me scared. I couldn't help it."

"Well, your treatment is not an instant fix, you know. You'll need a few weeks of work before it starts to set into your brains, um — I mean brain. Singular." Tim sighed and sat down behind his desk. He stared at a pencil, as if it might be a mythical God (a very small one) keen to give him the secrets of the universe.

"I wish Alan would come back." The strain was getting to the doctor. "He's much better at this sort of thing than me. I'm more of the *performer* in this practice. Why don't we get some marshmallows, eh? Invite the others up. Make an evening of it. Tell some stories round the old camp fire…"

"I don't think Agatha should really be sitting round a fire, do you?" said Paul.

"Ah, but marshmallows are really nice when you toast them," said Tim.

Paul started looking a bit purple again at the mention of the word toast. There was a knock at the door. Mrs Pincer walked in and with her wafted the screams of unruly behaviour coming from downstairs: the thick thud of sausages hitting walls.

"What am I supposed to do with the children?" She was exasperated. "It's chaos down there. Agatha is throwing lumps of mashed potato at Barry. Brenda is throwing sausages at Agatha. And Miriam is hiding under the table. Everything has gone to pot since Dr Alan disappeared. Where has he got to?"

Tim's daydream vanished into thin air – just like his brother had done. "Right, um, let's all go downstairs." Tim stopped just as he got to the door. "Who was the last person to see Alan?" he asked.

"I brought some sandwiches up for them at lunchtime," said the nurse.

"Them?"

Suddenly it clicked: Agatha. She had been the last person to see the doctor. They all raced downstairs, as if they were chickens and hungry foxes were snapping at their feet. When they got to the refectory, the scene before them was something to behold.

19. THE SCENE BEFORE THEM

Agatha was on the table, throwing bits of food at the other patients who were running round the refectory trying to dodge the missiles. M. Pipette ran up to Dr Tim.

"She's out of control, *non?*" he puffed. "She tried to knock me out so she could get hold of ze matches! Then she says she needs zem as part of her therapy! Of course I sez no, but then she starts throwing sausages at everyone! And they are premium meat!!"

M. Pipette's exclamation marks were fully justified.

"Agatha! Get down from there!" cried Tim.

Agatha didn't get off the table, but continued to throw things. Nurse Pincer tried her best.

"Agatha, my dear. Stop being quite so disturbed and get off that table like a good girl. There'll be plenty of marshmallows in it for you."

"I HATE MARSHMALLOWS!" shouted Agatha.

"LOOK, I'M THE ONE WHO SHOUTS ROUND HERE," Brenda hollered back. "I DON'T THINK IT'S FAIR THAT, AS WELL AS STANDING ON THE TABLE HAVING A TANTRUM, YOU SHOULD BE STEALING OTHER PATIENT'S PROBLEMS!"

"SHUT YOUR BIG FAT GOB!" screamed Agatha.

"Barry really thinks that you should not be talking to your fellow patient like that."

"AGATHA SAYS BARRY CAN SHUT UP TOO!" shrieked the horrendous child.

"Don't shout at Barry!" said Miriam, quieter than she had planned.

"BEEEEEEEEEEEE QUIEEEEEEEEEEEEEEETT!!!!!" The whole room fell silent. Everybody stared. For the first time in her life, Mrs Pincer had raised her voice.

She smiled and said to an astonished Agatha, "Let's get to the point, young lady. This is not a delightful situation. Where is Dr Alan? If you don't tell me now, then I shall drive you to a secret location and leave you there, where you will be prey to wolves and unwashed strangers. And I

*Agatha was on the table, throwing bits of food
at the other patients*

won't tell your parents where you are, either."

It was only at this point, when there was silence, that they all heard the muffled sound coming from the floor above. It sounded a bit like "lemon owl a hee".

"Alan!" shrieked Tim. And he ran upstairs, closely followed by everyone else. Nurse Pincer held onto Agatha's collar tightly as she led her upstairs, so she could not get up to any more tricks.

The sound was coming from the TRAGIC EVENTS ROOM. Tim opened the door to find his brother tied to a chair, his mouth gagged, wobbling around trying to break free. Tim untied the gag.

"Perhaps," said his brother, angrily. "It was tempting fate when we called this the TRAGIC EVENTS ROOM. I've been tied up for hours now. Did you not notice that I was gone?"

"Of course," said Tim. "I just thought you might have popped to the shops."

Alan ignored this.

"What have you done with Agatha? Have you punished her yet? That girl has some serious problems. She wanted to kidnap me, then set fire to this room. I thought I was a goner."

"Oh." Tim was speechless – well, for a moment. "Agatha!" he cried. Nurse Pincer nudged her forward. "You

Alan was tied to a chair, his mouth gagged,
wobbling around trying to break free

are going to need some... full-time therapy."

Agatha looked uninterested, because her appalling brain could never contemplate being nice.

Alan told everyone they could watch telly while he and his brother had a meeting. Agatha would have to sit on her own in the dormitory and consider what she had done (although perhaps this was unlikely).

"Will it be a crisis meeting?" asked Tim, wide-eyed.

"No," said Alan, elbowing his younger brother in the ribs.

"What was that thing about lemon owls?" Tim asked. "'*Lemon owl a hee!*' we heard you say."

"I was trying to shout, '*Let me out of here!*', you fool," said Alan.

"Not in front of the children," Tim replied. "Let's show professional unity."

20. THE MEETING, WHICH WAS DEFINITELY A CRISIS MEETING

"You can't just expel her; this is a clinic, not a school," said Tim when the brothers were alone in the INTER-VIEW ROOM. "She is here to get better. Where will she go if she can't stay at TreadQuietly?"

"She tried to murder me, Tim. She wanted to set fire to my legs; that's what she told me."

"At least it was only your legs."

"You really are a first-rate idiot sometimes." Alan was not in a good mood. Understandable, really: he had just been kidnapped by a twelve-year-old.

Alan described his morning with Agatha Bilke. In the

absence of Tim dressed up as firework (or indeed barbeque), Alan had sat her down in the TRAGIC EVENTS ROOM and let her watch the news. Such scenes of devastation and crime, he thought, might make her think about what damage she caused. It seemed to have the opposite effect. She had looked entranced by a story about a bomb going off in another country. Next, pictures of forest fires devouring homes and small business holdings had delighted the young girl. Later, Alan was sure he had seen a smile play upon her awful lips when there was an advert warning of the dangers of chip-pan fires. The thick carpet had helped to soak up the sound of Alan's screaming.

"She really is trouble, that one," he concluded. Not a medical diagnosis, but good enough all the same.

"I didn't think it would be this tough," sighed Tim. "I presumed we might get a few worried types in, scared of spiders, or a bit car-sick sometimes. But nothing like this. All the patients we've got are…"

"…Mental," finished Alan.

Tim looked at his brother. No psychologist would ever dare use that word. It was slang, offensive and misleading. However, Alan did have a point. They were surrounded by loonies. What on earth was society coming to? Could no one bring up their children without them being completely round the bend? No no, he thought, they must be kind.

"Agatha needs us," said Tim, calmly. "She is crying out for help."

"No, that was *me*, remember. Stuck in that room. But you didn't bother to find me for a few weeks, did you? What a great doctor you are." As if it were contagious, Alan was now using sarcasm just as Agatha might.

Tim continued regardless. "If we can save Agatha from herself…"

"If we can save ourselves from Agatha, more to the point," Alan grimaced.

"…Then we will put this Clinic on the map! We shall be highly respected worldwide and we might win the Nobel Peace Prize, or even the Best Doctors in the World Award!"

Alan simply turned to look out of the window. He need not comment on Tim's vivid imagination at this precise second.

"We shall cure Agatha!" Tim was triumphant. "We shall cure all our patients at TreadQuietly. Even the really mad ones!!!"

"But first," interrupted Alan. "We must remember that when we are dealing with Agatha Bilke, we must both be with her, together, never just one of us. We may have to

There was a knock on the door and Paul walked in,
with some trepidation

raise Pipette's wages if we have to, but he must always guard those matches. She nearly got them just now: under no circumstances can we have Agatha starting a fire."

There was a knock on the door and Paul walked in, with some trepidation.

"Excuse me, Doctors Humphrey," he said. "But I am appealing to you on behalf of the children here at TreadQuietly. We think Agatha has gone too far."

"Well yes, fine, but we're the grown-ups round here so we make the rules." Dr Alan tried to hurry Paul out of the door.

"No, let him speak," said Tim. "What is it you wanted to say, Paul?"

"I have an idea," said the sensitive youngster. "A way in which we can let Agatha know she can't get away with this sort of behaviour in the Clinic."

"Really?" Alan was a mixture of surprise and disbelief.

"I don't think we, the patients, can do this. Brenda can't keep quiet, and everyone else lacks the... authority. But..."

Together, Paul and the doctors hatched a plan.

21. AGATHA ALONE – *GULP*

If you were one the few quite deranged people in the world (yes, yes, see the back page if you need help), you might think that locking Agatha in the dormitory would be an ideal way to calm her down. There, she could not throw sausages at anyone, or tie a doctor to a chair. She would be no trouble at all.

And that, to the outside observer, is exactly what happened. Agatha sat on her bed, leafing through a book about the disappearance of the rainforest, looking calm and collected. She was not trying to rub sticks together to make a flame, nor was she putting toast in Paul's shoes.

But she was quietly seething that she could not spend the

evening watching television with the others. All right, so she had a few issues to resolve and was being punished, but didn't Barry always talk about Barry? Didn't Brenda always shout? None of the other children had been cured – which made them the same as Agatha: they were all patients here. So why was she locked up on her own, straining to hear the sound of a TV movie in the other room?

It simply didn't make sense and it wasn't fair – they were probably all stuffing their gobs with marshmallows, too.

She heard noises from the TV seeping in under the door and through the walls. The hero was trying to save the world. Cars were bumping into things. The evil dictator had worked out the hero's weak spot in order to defeat him.

That was it! The weak spot. Dr Tim would have been pleased, dear readers, for Agatha had for the first time in her life empathised – but at this point it was with a villain, not a "good guy". In the Clinic, Agatha was in the perfect place – she was surrounded by weak spots. Paul, Miriam, Barry, Brenda... they were one big Achilles heel. If there was one thing she had bothered to learn at school, it was that Achilles had a rubbish foot.

Having realised this, Agatha knew it would be easy to watch the TreadQuietly Clinic and all its inhabitants burn down in a shock of flames. All she had do was cause a distraction, deflecting attention away from herself while she got M. Pipette's matches. Doing the opposite, i.e. throwing mashed potato at the others was never going to work, she realised that now. She congratulated herself: she was becoming a proper little criminal mastermind. If she wasn't going to get any marshmallows (she had lied when she told Mrs Pincer she didn't like them), she'd see these people got their come-uppance.

To start with, it would not be difficult to send Miriam into a panic. Just telling her that a meteorite – no, better still, two – were headed for earth would require the doctors to use all their expertise to calm her down. That was three people dealt with already.

Next, when Paul realised that there was a piece of toast stuck to the back of his jumper, he too would be paralysed with fear and unable to save them. Mrs Pincer would have to deal with him. Another two down.

She stopped for a moment. Why hadn't she thought of this before? Agatha felt a warm glow of wickedness run through her veins, like the feeling you get when you've had a mug of very chocolatey hot chocolate on a cold winter's day (although obviously this feeling is ridiculous and you must not be inclined to think evil thoughts in the future in the hope it will be just like drinking a

smashing cup of cocoa).

Resuming her diabolical plan, Agatha decided she need only whisper something controversial to Brenda and she would shout it out to everybody. A carefully screamed, "I HEAR DOCTOR ALAN AND DOCTOR TIM ARE QUALIFIED FOR NOTHING MORE THAN FIXING TOILETS!!" would mean that M. Pipette would be too busy shutting her up to watch his matches.

Lastly, Barry. All you would have to do would be to ask him to recite the alphabet and watch him get stuck like a broken record. "A, b, c, d, e, f, g, h, Barry – er, Barry – er, Barry – oops, Barry… um…" Ooh, how splendid it all was. How splendid in a sickening, horrifying, gruesome dictator sort of way.

The children would be too incapacitated by fear to fight the hideous flames that would lead to their destruction. The adults would be tending to the children first and the blaze would rage out of control before they could do anything about it – let's face it, everyone here was really quite pathetic. The fire would, she reckoned, spread quickly into the council's fridge mountain. Agatha knew that fridges were filled with flammable gases. It would be like a bomb going off, her finest piece of work to date. She would be able to escape and then become a threat to the whole of humanity. How wonderful.

What she had not reckoned on was that Paul might be trying to think of ways in which to make her behave. Surely he was too busy being sick to think about anything that might save this so-called Clinic? Agatha believed that, as Miriam had remarked, she was invincible.

She heard the key in the lock, saw the handle turn and Mrs Pincer walked in. Agatha sat up straight; surely Mrs Pincer could not have heard what she was thinking? Of course not. Impossible.

"There's someone here to see you, Agatha," she said, nervously, as she ushered a visitor in. "This is Inspector Coddles," she announced.

The Inspector stood and narrowed his eyes at her.

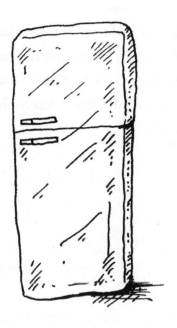

Agatha knew that fridges were filled with flammable gases

22. AN INSPECTOR CALLS

The Inspector wore a trilby hat and a big trench-coat over a smart suit. He looked like he had spent his life narrowing his eyes. "Agatha Bilke," he said, somewhat obviously, for there was no one else in the room.

"Yes," said Agatha.

"Inspector Coddles, New Scotland Yard."

"What do you want?" asked the errant child.

"I hear you had a few problems before you came to the Clinic," said Coddles, walking slowly towards Agatha. "I hear you attended St Heavy Workloads' School and during the time you were there the building 'accidentally' caught fire and everything went up in smoke."

The inspector looked like he had spent his life
narrowing his eyes

Agatha said nothing.

"And I hear your sister suffered on her wedding day when the family found her dress had been left in a shed which had – again – 'accidentally' caught fire. I haven't even started on the canoes."

Agatha was not quivering, nor was she shaking. She had spoken to police officers before and she knew what it was like. They were always stating the obvious, not expecting you to answer back, always standing up when you were sitting down.

"I've heard a few tales from this place, you know," said Inspector Coddles, flaring his nostrils and breathing in deeply, with a slight hissing sound. "There are neighbours. They hear things. They see things. They smell thin –"

Inspector Coddles's well-worn speech was interrupted as he heard the door-handle turn. Perhaps Mrs Pincer – a delightful lady, it must be said, fine features, rosy cheeks – had thought to bring him a pot of tea and some caramel Hobnobs.

So few people were thoughtful in this day and age, Coddles mused, the old values were all but gone. Take the specimen in front of him, for example. A very rude girl who had no respect for others, or the law. An example of the arrogance of the modern age.

"Excuse me," came the voice from behind the door. "Agatha Bilke?"

It was not Mrs Pincer. In place of the delightful, middle-aged nurse was a man in a trilby hat, wearing a big trench-coat over a smart suit. The only visible difference between him and Inspector Coddles was that he wore a badly-trimmed moustache. He also seemed to make a scuttling noise when he walked in the room, as if a young child were hurrying in behind him, to hide in a corner and watch cvents.

23. ANOTHER INSPECTOR CALLS

"Inspector Noddles, New Sco—" announced the new inspector, narrowing his eyes.

Then he noticed that Agatha already had company. Neither he nor Paul, who was trying to remain unobtrusive in the corner, had expected this.

The two inspectors stared at each other, as if they had never seen another human being before. Of course, they were quite old so they had seen loads, but they were both in shock.

"Who are you?" asked Inspector Noddles.

"Inspector Coddles. And you?"

"Inspector Noddles."

"Is there a problem?" Agatha asked both men, delighting in the confusion.

"Which station do you work for?" asked Coddles. "I thought *we* were dealing with Agatha."

"Erm…" Noddles looked worried. "I'm a… private investigator."

Coddles looked distrustful.

"I call myself Inspector," Noddles continued. "Because I used to be, when I was in the Police force. Force of habit, ha ha!"

Coddles didn't laugh.

"I was just having a word with Agatha," said Coddles, try-ing to shoo Noddles back out of the door. "If you don't mind…"

What was Noddles to do? He also wanted a word with the girl. "Could I not just sit in and listen?" he asked, being nosey (as he was supposed to be).

"No, this is highly confidential," warned Coddles, as ferocious as a ferret who's just trodden on a hairbrush.

Mrs Pincer walked in with a pot of tea and some biscuits on a plate. She stopped in her tracks as she spotted the new Inspector. "Oh, er, hello Sir. I'll, um, go and get another cup." Then she gave Noddles a funny look, as if she recognised him, and walked out. She did not see Paul, who

Another inspector calls

was as baffled as everyone else.

Who was this other chap? Paul wondered. He was certainly very serious. Big moustache. Full of authority. Paul hoped these inspectors hadn't blown his plan. He prayed that "Noddles" would try to remain calm and this Coddles wouldn't get too suspicious. He listened to the two men trying to deal with Agatha as he sat tight against the bed, gazing down at the floor. It hadn't been vacuumed recently.

"Looks like I'll have to stay, then." Noddles tried to sound defiant, so he wouldn't appear nervous. He was making this up as he went along, and he wasn't used to it. "Perhaps I can help you with a little insider information, which I have gathered from my work on this case in the last few weeks," he spluttered.

"Oh yes?" Coddles thought he might as well let this Noddles chap do all the work.

"Yes." Noddles shifted about on his feet. "Er, I am here specifically to tell Miss Agatha Bilke that she has been quite difficult up to now – according to reports – and that if she continues she will be, um, severely punished by the promising young therapists that run this, er, TreadQuietly Clinic For Interesting Children.

"And furthermore," Noddles was now in his stride.

"Agatha Bilke will be arrested and detained for at least, um, four years if she ever causes havoc like she did at teatime. It's official. Scared, Agatha?"

Agatha's suspicions that Inspector Noddles was Dr Tim Humphrey in full acting mode were confirmed. The doctor was trying to intimidate her – little realising that she could not be intimidated, and especially not by an officer of the law. She presumed (rightly) that Inspector Coddles was a real inspector and that the Humphrey brothers had not – at least Tim hadn't – been informed of his arrival. Agatha would have tried to pat herself on the back for this clever deduction had she:

a) not been in company and

b) not known it was physically impossible to do so.

But Agatha had not realised that Paul was hiding in the room.

"Arrrreuuoooooghhhhhh!" came the sound from the corner. Paul had spotted something. He leapt up, looking horrified.

"That toast she put in my bed is still on the floor!" he continued, pointing at Agatha, explaining the facts in case anyone was not aware what his problem was.

Paul was beset by anxiety again – this time due to an oversight rather than malice. No one had meant for the toast to be on the floor, they had merely forgotten about it. Agatha smiled a little, because she liked to watch Paul suffer, whatever the occasion.

But this time, it was Paul that had changed. As he tried to calm his breathing, and "Noddles" danced in front of him singing the song about teapots, he gave Agatha a look of such utter contempt and acidic rage, that for the first time she felt her reign of chaos might be threatened. Paul had had enough. He hated Agatha.

"The TreadQuietly Clinic is full of loonies," thought Inspector Coddles, as he watched the strange scene.

"I really am enjoying this role, it's such fun," thought Tim.

"Sorry to interrupt, Inspector," asked Coddles, tired and confused. "But could I see one of the Humphrey doctors?"

"I'll be back... I think," Tim warned Agatha, as they left the dormitory and locked the terrible child back in there.

24. A MEETING WHICH TURNED OUT NOT TO BE A CRISIS MEETING

Tim tried to explain all in the EXPLANATIONS ROOM (which looked strangely like the INTERVIEW ROOM, though Coddles wasn't to know). This was a new kind of therapy, Tim told Coddles, fusing drama and traditional methods of treatment. It was going to be a wow with every youngster who's ever had difficulty eating pears in public or looking at snails, for instance. He'd seen for his own eyes that Paul, who was now with Nurse Pincer, was a tricky case – but he could be cured and he would be cured!

Alan was tiring of listening to a speech he'd heard many times before and wanted to get to the bottom of things.

Why was Inspector Coddles making unannounced visits?

"We are doing very well in the Clinic," he told the policeman. "We are unaware that we need police involvement."

"I was just following up leads, Dr Humphrey," said Coddles, narrowing his eyes. TreadQuietly certainly was an odd place. This room, for instance, was so white it was like standing in the North Pole.

"Leads?" asked Alan. "Agatha has only been here for a few days, she hasn't had time to go out and cause havoc."

"Just standard police procedure," said Coddles.

"Have you got everything you need?" sighed Alan. "You can see Agatha is perfectly fine and not causing any mischief in here. We are law-abiding persons in this Clinic. We are not crazy scientists who care nothing for rules and regulations. We have a TV licence and everything."

"Glad to hear it. By the way, is that fridge mountain in the back garden legal?" asked Coddles, narrowing his eyes further, which was some feat. (Heaven knows what his feet were doing.)

"Yes, the back garden is council property," said Alan.

"All right, fair enough," said Coddles. Then, softening a little, "I must say, I was a little bewildered earlier on, but I am satisfied with what I've seen. And, I admit, your methods of therapy sound very interesting indeed. I am only sorry for troubling you and Agatha. I hope she finds herself in a much better frame of mind soon, for all our sakes. But," and he sighed. "I ought to inform you that I will be keeping an eye on this place, it's only my duty. She's done some dreadful things in her time, Agatha has... I will see myself out."

Coddles left the room. Tim, still dressed as Inspector Noddles, took off his trilby, sat down and ripped the false moustache from his upper lip. Alan spoke.

"So there was a Coddles *and* a Noddles who visited Agatha?" said Alan, wearily. "We can't seem to get anything right. She'll be the death of us, that girl." (Oh! And how she wished it!)

"Mrs Pincer let him in, I had no idea he was there," said Tim. "But Agatha was probably doubly scared by seeing two officers of the law. That's the thing, bro', her parents have not given her a strict enough upbringing. She has been allowed to do what she wants. Here, she is under lock and key, she is watched constantly, she will be treated daily.

She *must* behave. And then…"

"…I know," said Alan wearily. "We'll win the Best Doctors in the World Award."

"And then we can have a disco and Dowdie and The Bears can play!"

"Who?"

"Just a band I like," said Tim, meekly.

"Paul really wants to help us cure Agatha," said Alan, changing the subject. "This is all very serious."

"It certainly is," said his brother. "I wonder if he's got any more plans…?"

"Now now. We can't expect our patients to do our work for us. No more hare-brained schemes, Tim."

"Still, eh? Paul could become the saviour of humanity if he sorts out Agatha! Just think! She'd be nice, we'd be happy, and he could win the Best Doctors…"

"Let's just get these therapies in place first, Tim. *We'll* be the ones to cure Agatha."

Alan was less confident than he appeared. Had he known what would happen the next morning he might have decided to leave TreadQuietly there and then. For good.

25. AGATHA'S MIND

Of course, Agatha was not "doubly scared" by Tim and Inspector Coddles. She was doubly confident. She had been moved to a separate dormitory and this only seemed to give her more status as a leading practitioner of menace. But had she not entertained doubt when she last looked into Paul's eyes, we ask? Yes, but it had now gone. What could a shivering wreck like Paul do to her? Agatha, it will sadden you to read, thought she was winning. She was more determined than ever to beat Paul now that he was spying on her. The traitor.

She had amassed more materials. Not only did she have the hat and various bits of wood and paper, she had some scraps of papier-maché that Tim had discarded when making props. She had also stolen four bags of marsh-mallows — everything else could be "borrowed".

Those thick carpets at TreadQuietly — they made running down to the kitchens so easy, she was never heard!

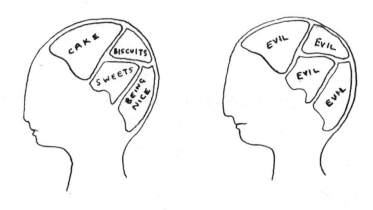

Normal mind   **Agatha's mind**

If only she could get those matches! Calm down, said Agatha's mind to Agatha, it will not be difficult. M. Pipette may be guarding them with his life, but you will find a way.

Agatha listened and thought she could hear the sound of the others in the next room sleeping. Three noses breathing in, three noses breathing out and Barry snoring. What poor defenceless creatures they were, wrapped up in their own troubles. They were too strange to cope with the real world, too peculiar to be with other children. Even Paul, who was trying so hard to conquer his fear, had not imagined Agatha might be so great, so resilient.

She would play the real world on its own terms, she would not cower or slink away. She was more real than those wan souls who hoped that TreadQuietly might offer them a cure.

She smiled one of those smiles of hers and remembered that she had not cleaned her teeth, but she did not care. She was too excited about the day ahead. The children would not have a chance! What an awful child.

26. PAUL'S MIND

Paul lay awake, wondering what to do next. Agatha was misbehaving.

She had put toast in his bed, thrown food at everyone, kidnapped Dr Alan, repeatedly laughed at his misfortune, and this evening Mrs Pincer had told him that there were four bags of marshmallows unaccounted for.

Paul had never hated anyone before, not really, but it felt easy and right to despise Agatha so much. It wasn't like hating marzipan, or mauve, both of which would never fight back. Agatha was trouble, and she would fight back — in the best way she could.

Of course, Agatha must be planning a fire. She would

never be happy simply taunting everyone, if her past history was anything to go by. Paul didn't know if he could stand up to such devastation. After all, he was not super-human. He was a boy who was scared of toast.

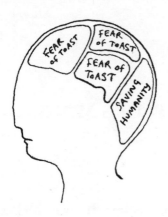

Paul's mind

He thought about the world: the leaves on the trees, the grass in the park – he even grew fond remembering the fridges sitting in TreadQuietly's back garden. This planet was a lovely place, full of joy, full of marshmallows, full of... hope. (The more cynical among you might say it was full of toast, too, but let's forget about that for one second.) Why did Agatha want to destroy all the goodness that life could bring?

Paul must stop Agatha, stop her from causing so much destruction. If she won now, she might go on to threaten the future of humanity.

But things aren't always as simple as that.

Are they?

27. A DELIGHTFUL MORNING

The children awoke the following day to a fine morning. Mrs Pincer, of course, described it as delightful. Once dressed, they hopped downstairs to a lovely breakfast of oaty cereal and chocolate milk. What a wonderful place this was, full of nice food and friendly adults; people who cared, who wanted to heal them with kind words and amateur dramatics. Now Agatha had been visited by the police, many of the children thought that everything was going to be all right.

Brenda tucked into her cereal and yodelled. "I REALLY DO THINK THAT WITHIN THE NEXT TWO WEEKS THESE TREATMENTS WILL REALLY START TO

WORK!! I'M SURE I'M A LOT LESS LOUDER THAN I WAS YESTERDAY!!"

"Barry would so love to be like everyone else too," said Barry, finishing his drink.

"The day I take off this silly metal hat," added Miriam, "won't be a day too soon."

Paul nodded. He, too, wanted to get rid of his stupid phobia. He quickly shot a glance at Agatha, who smirked. He knew she was up to something but he thought he was now prepared for it.

Oh reader. Dear, sweet, loyal reader. Look at brave Paul! He was ready to fight – whatever hour, day or week. He had placed a wet tea-towel in his bag so he always had it handy to smother a fire. He had decided to wear Wellingtons in the hope that they might give added protection. But most of all, he was mentally prepared. He expected Agatha to strike (quite literally) at any time. He would not falter. Never. He was on guard.

He did not know, as he sat with the other children, that Agatha had already been at work.

A damp tea-towel was no use. A fire extinguisher would not have helped either. Agatha had already pinned a piece of toast to the back of Paul's jumper – and when he found out he would go to pieces because the Humphreys had not cured him yet.

No one, as yet, had noticed it.

"Did you hear the news this morning?" asked Agatha, wiping her mouth with a paper napkin. "Two meteorites are heading towards the earth. They should get here by this afternoon. They're very big and might well wipe out a continent... probably Europe."

Miriam looked at Agatha. Miriam turned white. Then Miriam turned blue. Then Miriam let out a scream, which many would describe as "almighty", but here we shall describe as:

"Aaaaaaaaaaaaaaaaaarrrrrrrrrrrrgeughhhhhhhhhhh!!"

Miriam's breath was quick and shallow. She dived to the floor.

"Dr Tim! Dr Alan! Meteorites are headed this way!!!"

The doctors ran into the refectory and tried to calm Miriam. As this kerfuffle ensued, Agatha whispered something to Brenda. The girl, as predicted, blurted it out immediately – and noisily.

"I HEAR THE HUMPHREY BROTHERS ARE ONLY QUALIFIED TO, ER– WHAT WAS IT AGAIN??"

Agatha whispered again into Brenda's ear.

"YEAH, THAT'S RIGHT. THEY'RE ONLY QUALI-FIED TO BE DOCTORS!!!"

"No, that's not right!" said Agatha. "They're *not* qualified to be doctors. That's the point, don't you see?"

"NO, NOT REALLY!!!!!!" shouted Brenda, as M. Pipette fussed around her, telling her to be quiet. Agatha left them for a moment and walked up to Barry.

"Recite the alphabet, Barry, please..."

True to form, he could only mutter "A, b, c, d, e, f, g, h, Barry – er, Barry – er, Barry – oops, Barry... um..."

Agatha surveyed the scene: Dr Alan Humphrey patting Miriam on the head, Paul holding her hand, Tim looking as if he was going to faint himself (useless!), and M. Pipette still trying to calm Brenda – although she was shouting about how *qualified* the doctors were and not the other way around, she was still causing a disturbance. Needless to say, Barry was still stuck on the alphabet.

Mrs Pincer rushed in from the carpark. This would be it, thought Agatha. Pincer would spot the toast on Paul's back, he'd go nuts and the chaos would be complete. Then Agatha could steal the matches and set fire to the bundle of flammables she had arranged in the corner of the refectory. The whole place would explode, thanks to the CFCs in the fridges and there was nothing that anyone could do about it. Radiators, cufflinks and bones would be all that was left. Inspector Coddles had never expected anything as grand as this. And where was he now? Nowhere. Ha!

"Aaaaaaooooooooorrrruuughhhh! Paul!" screamed Nurse Pincer as she spotted the toast on Paul's back. "Don't look, my lovely, I just have to take this little... thing off you..."

"What is it?" asked Paul, trying to twist round to see.

"Nothing, sweetkins," said Pincer, ripping the toast off and trying to hide it.

Agatha ran to the kitchen and seized the matches. No one spotted her until it was too late – she had caused a rumpus all right. She ran to the corner of the room, struck the match and set light to the pile of wood, paper and marshmallows. She turned round to the assembled mess of people and shouted, in her best impression of Brenda,

"NOW I'M *REALLY* GOING TO TOAST SOME MARSHMALLOWS! THIS IS THE END FOR THE TREADQUIETLY CLINIC FOR INTERESTING CHILDREN!! JUST YOU WAIT TILL THE FIRE SPREADS TO THE FRIDGE MOUNTAIN!!! HA HA!!! GOODBYE, PEOPLE, IT'S BEEN ER, NOT VERY NICE KNOWING YOU!!!!" and with that she ran out of the door and locked it behind her.

28. OH DEAR

For a moment, no one moved. The group was in complete shock, every last one of them – "last" being the operative word.

Mrs Pincer was so surprised that she dropped the piece of toast she was supposed to be hiding from Paul, and he saw it, sitting there on the floor.

She looked at the boy. She waited for his reaction. The whole room stopped and stared at Paul, waiting for his howls of despair, knowing this would be the last straw.

Paul looked at the slice intently, for the doctors' sake, for everyone's sake. Paul was trying to *become* the toast. Just an innocent slice of bread that was sitting on the floor while the Clinic was about to burn down with all the people in it.

Tim looked at the child. "Go on, Paul!" he shouted. "You can do it! It's only a little piece of toast!!"

"Aaaaaaaargggghhhh!" cried Paul. But this was not an "Aaaaaaaargggghhhh!" of fear. This was an "Aaaaaa-aargggghhhh!" of power, of conquering your problems because there's the incey-wincey fact that a raging fire is

*Paul was trying to **become** the toast*

about to engulf you and everyone else at any moment. Paul could not let everyone expire.

"Aaaaaaaarggggghhhh!" said Paul again, just for luck and stamped on the piece of toast. "Ha ha!" he laughed. "Come on everyone! We can fight this! Stop dithering and let's put this darned fire out before we die!"

He dragged Miriam up off the floor.

"Get the bucket and start filling it with water," he said, commandingly. She didn't move.

"Miriam, there are no meteorites headed this way!"

She quickly got up and did what she was told.

"Doctors, Pincer and Pipette – get every jug or pan and fill them up and throw water at the fire. Brenda, shout for help. But everyone, especially the adults, lie low because we don't want the smoke to get us!"

Paul looked at Barry. He was still stuck on the alphabet. "And Barry, you hold this damp tea-towel as back-up and make sure everyone's co-ordinated." It didn't matter that Barry's job was a bit vague, thought Paul, as long as he felt involved.

After a long few minutes throwing

water around and ducking down to avoid the smoke, the team started to bring the fire under control. (Paul's wellies were actually quite useful in the end.)

They heard the door-handle rattle on the other side and then a voice from behind it shouted, "Charge!!!"

The door wobbled a bit, then fell off its hinges to reveal Inspector Coddles standing before them, his trilby hat askew but his eyes still narrow.

"I heard the shouting," he puffed. "What's going on in here?"

"You're a bit late," said Paul. "Agatha Bilke tried to set TreadQuietly – including us – on fire."

"That fridge mountain would have added to things," said Coddles. "Nasty. I better get on to the council to remove it. It's a hazard."

"Thanks, Coddles," said Dr Tim, dusting his white coat with his hands. He turned round to everyone. "Phew, it's been a bit of a morning."

29. THE BEST DOCTORS IN THE WORLD AWARD

Tim looked at the mess around him and spotted the piece of toast that was still on the floor. He tried to edge it away with his foot. He didn't know if Paul was going to have a panic attack this time – his immense bravery was probably just a blip.

"No, it's all right," said Paul, who noticed what the doctor was doing. "I'm not afraid anymore."He stooped down and picked up the slice, took a mouthful and smiled. (Well, actually he didn't bite into it, because it had been trodden on quite a lot and was pretty disgusting. But he would have done if it had been fresh and not on the floor, for Paul's fear had disappeared.)

"I really think we should all go outside and get some proper air," said Barry.

"Me too," said Brenda and they followed Coddles outside to the carpark. Miriam took off her corrugated-iron hat and scratched her head.

"It really is a delightful morning, isn't it?" she said, as she looked at the bright blue sky, hat still in her hand.

"Yes, but never mind that," said Alan. "We've always got work to do. You're not going to get better on your own, are you?"

"No, it's all right," said Paul, "I'm not afraid anymore"

Tim nudged Alan.

"What are you doing?" said the older Humphrey. "Stop it!"

"Didn't you hear what our patients – our ex-patients – just said?" asked Tim. "Didn't you watch what they just did?"

"They're cured!" Coddles butted in. "Good Lord! That's amazing!"

"Hang on, I must pick you up on one point. I thought you said that we're cured..." said Barry. "Oh my goodness! He's right!"

Miriam felt the top of her head, with no hat. She started to giggle.

"We're cured! He's right! Listen to me!" said Brenda, talking and not shouting for the first time.

Alan stood, dumbfounded. "I guess it was the shock of the fire," he said. "It's a miracle."

"Shock of the fire or not," said Coddles. "This will put you on the map. Not even here for one week and all these Interesting Children are saved from their Interesting Problems!"

"Now we can continue our pioneering work for ever! The Humphrey Technique will save people left, right and centre!" shrieked Tim, hugging his brother. "And we'll get even more awards!"

"I think this is cause for celebration," said Coddles. "Why

don't you get back inside, arrange a party and I'll get some of my friends from the local press to come along and report on the whole marvellous event."

"And Dowdie and the Bears can come and play!"

"Well, I'm not sure I can get them," admitted Coddles. "But one of the chaps back at the station has got a drum machine so I can promise you some breakdancing."

"Just one thing," Paul piped up. "Where's Agatha?"

Everyone looked at everyone else. Eyes flitted around as if they were watching flies play Ping-Pong.

"Er, don't you worry," said Coddles, who hadn't narrowed his eyes for at least five minutes. "I'm sure we'll track her down. We're the police, you know."

30. THE END

Coddles found Agatha; it didn't take long. She was standing across the road, waiting for the great blaze; waiting for her sickening reign of awfulness to begin anew and *really* affect the future of humanity etc, etc.

Coddles put a firm hand on her shoulder and told her she was wanted down the station.

Paul and the other children had their party, got their pictures in the local paper and eventually on the national TV news. They went home to their parents, joyfully rid of their former woes. Paul picked up a special prize for *Bravest Child* on TV's *Great! Kids!* show. He was especially pleased with his trophy, and put it on his bookshelf at home. It

reminded him of that difficult last day at TreadQuietly (the trophy, not the bookshelf) and all the difficult days before it, but it made him happy because he'd conquered that little (and peculiarly large) bit of fear he thought he'd be stuck with forever.

The TreadQuietly Clinic became a popular and successful therapy centre; the Humphrey Technique was now world-famous. Children – including Kim Dolphin and her imaginary friend Bonce – came from far and wide to be treated. And, although they never saw quite as speedy a recovery as those children in that first week, the Humphrey brothers' new-found confidence saw that, eventually, their unique methods worked a treat.

And Dowdie and the Bears? When they saw the Clinic on the news, they sent a floral bouquet to Tim and Alan, congratulating them on their work and promising they'd play there whenever they were asked. From then on, every Christmas, former and existing patients were invited to one humdinging party where they ate marshmallows and hopped to the sounds of everyone's favourite band. Oh, and Mrs Pincer and M.Pipette were married the next spring. It was a lovely occasion; even Bonce enjoyed himself and managed not to hit his head once.

Agatha never set foot in TreadQuietly ever again, but Coddles gave her parents a list of more traditional therapists and she received some help. Did she get any better? Well, that's the question. For girls like Agatha who are absolutely awful, it takes time to rid them of their wicked thoughts and even more wicked deeds. Could Agatha become a good and useful person? Sorry to disappoint you, but it is simply too early to tell.

*Mrs Pincer and M. Pipette were
married the next spring. It was a lovely occasion*

BACK PAGE

As promised, something about the word "committed" (and all those other references to, um, things):

It's all about being a bit, er… and then, hmmm…

When you start to think of yourself as a dragon, people get a bit worried.

Wah wah wooh wooh boing boing boing.

Editor's note: the writer is taking a long, well-earned break on the South coast for rest and relaxation. Please do not bother the writer any more, or mention the words "restrained" or "sound mind" anywhere near the Bournemouth area. Thank you.

Siân Pattenden has been a journalist for a few years, working for titles including *Smash Hits*, *NME*, *The Face* and the *Guardian*. She has also been on the telly and radio. She is married to songwriter Luke Haines and has a son called Fred. They live in London.